I0574290

NORTH BY NORTH POLE *Beach*

A Christmas
Novella

KIMBERLY KURTH GRAY

Year of the Book
135 Glen Avenue
Glen Rock, PA 17327

ISBN: 978-1-64649-304-3 (print)
ISBN: 978-1-64649-305-0 (ebook)

Chapter 1

At breakfast on Tuesday, Mrs. Doolittle announced she had found the perfect job for me.

"And not just any old job, dearie..." she said in that squeaky helium-filled voice of hers, "...one that could turn into a permanent position." The deepening of her cheek dimples revealed how pleased she was with herself.

I pushed aside my plate of blueberry waffles, usually a dish I favored. My spirits now were as drippy as the butter melting over my meal. "I already have a job," I said, more defensively than I'd intended, then took a deep breath. "There's still four more days work at Dolle's, and one of the waitresses at Robin Hood Restaurant is sure to go on maternity soon. She looks as if she may pop. They will definitely be ringing up the temp agency for help."

Mrs. Doolittle sighed, causing one of her haphazardly pinned red curls to slide down, the bobby pin dangling close to her eye. "Now, Natalie, haven't we had this same discussion before, dear?"

We had, more than once over the three years since I'd moved to Rehoboth Beach. Mrs. Doolittle had given me a job at The Doolittle Temp Agency the day I drove into town. Fortunately for me, it included a room in her boarding house. I'd had no place to go and little money after my second marriage went bust. Technically the rascal was my first husband, but that's another story.

Driving down to the beach to console myself that day had been the best decision I'd made in... well, probably the only good decision I'd ever made, if I was honest. My life in New York was a mess and going to Mom's in Baltimore was a last resort. After a few days with her, I needed a change of scenery. Meeting Violet Doolittle transformed my plans from a day trip to a new way of life. I'd become comfortable here, and, truth be told, I was afraid of venturing out and away, afraid that would lead to me making yet another mistake.

"Pass it along to the new girl... what's-her-name," I said and rethought the waffles as my stomach growled in hunger.

"I think you may be very interested in this job, though," Mrs. Doolittle persisted as she nudged my plate closer.

"I don't think so," I said and stabbed the fork into a square glistening with real maple syrup.

Mrs. Doolittle sat heavily into the chair next to me and smiled like the cat who ate the fattest canary. Her green eyes shone brightly, and her dimples deepened. "You will never guess who the client is." She waited for my reply, but I was hesitant to play this game.

"Oh, alright," I finally said because she looked as if she might explode with excitement. "Just tell me who this wonderous mystery client is before you burst."

"The job is with..." Mrs. Doolittle milked it like the announcer of a game show. "...Mrs. North." She clapped her hands gleefully as the name spilled from her lips.

"Mrs. North?" The fork clanged against my plate. "*The* Mrs. North? The reclusive Mrs. North who writes the advice column for the *Beach Banner*?"

Mrs. Doolittle's head nodded so quickly I feared it might roll off her shoulders. "Yes, yes, that very same one. Her butler, or husband, or, well I'm not sure who he was, but some man called early this morning to say that Mrs. North required an assistant. That's how he put it... 'required.' She's very fancy, you know."

"She won't want me, Mrs. Doolittle. Once she hears my name, or sees my face, she'll know who I am. I'm not the one for this job." I once again pushed the plate away, my appetite completely deserting me.

"It's perfect for you, Natalie. Penny, the new girl—or what's-her-name, as you so fondly refer to her—is not qualified. I pride myself in sending out the best people for the job. I have my reputation to consider, dearie. Penny is a hard worker, from what I've seen, and she'll do fine at the candy counter or serving meals, but you are the only one I have with the right background."

For over twenty years I'd worked as a personal assistant, seventeen of them for an actress. When I'd been hired by Lady M, she was working on a daytime drama and doing local dinner theater. By the time we parted ways, three years ago, I had two hundred dollars, a car, and a tattered reputation. She had her stardom and my husband. Lady M bad-mouthed me to any and everyone who would listen, and I played into her drama. The photo of me slapping her was front page news across the country. I was told no one wanted to hire an emotional woman like me.

"Mrs. North won't want me," I repeated.

"She will and she does. In fact, she expects you at her house at ten." Mrs. Doolittle checked her watch. "Which means you have less than an hour to ready yourself and get there."

I opened my mouth to argue, but Mrs. Doolittle shook her head. "Not another word, Natalie. Mrs. North is expecting you. She knows your name and says you are the exact person she wants. I spoke to her when she called to confirm not five minutes before you came down the stairs. Don't let me down," she said before standing. When she reached the kitchen doorway, Mrs. Doolittle turned. "More importantly, Natalie, don't let yourself down."

The walk from the Doolittle boarding house to Stockley Street took me a good twenty minutes. I crossed the bridge and admired Silver Lake. I knew it was important to arrive on time, but my feet dragged slower with each step. I wished I was behind the counter at Dolle's making conversation with Miss Hardy when she came in for her morning toffee that she liked to have with her coffee.

The October morning sky was bright, and everything was quiet now that children were back in school and most tourists had returned to their daily lives. This was my favorite time of year at the beach. An osprey flew overhead, and I shielded my eyes from the sun to watch him careen into the clouds then gently glide down to the sand.

The house, Mrs. North's house, was now to my left. The Silver Lake area was not one I was overly familiar with, though I did come by occasionally to see the famed Shell House. Mrs. North's old weathered gray house sat on a corner lot and was one of the original properties, though not as large as the du Pont's 7,800 square-foot "cottage." I'd passed her home a few times since living here, only discovering recently who lived inside. Its salt-stained shingles and worn bricks were as foreboding as Mrs. North herself was rumored to be. But who could say for sure? Not one person I knew had ever admitted to meeting her, and the few who claimed to have glimpsed her from the beach had difficulty even remembering what she looked like.

I made my way around the high seagrass to the front door and stood for a few seconds before ringing the bell. There was still time to turn back. I could say no one answered the door. Maybe this was a prank. Mrs. Doolittle might believe that. After all, before this morning she'd never spoken to Mrs. North. The woman on the other end of the line could have been anyone. But then I thought of Mrs. Doolittle's sweet round face and the brightness in her eyes and knew I couldn't disappoint her. She'd been more than kind to me over the years and having Mrs. North as a client was a big deal for the agency. I wouldn't let her down.

My fist was positioned to knock when the door flew open and a tall man with long white hair and a white, close-trimmed beard came barreling out. His tightly fit wetsuit left little to the imagination.

He didn't stop to greet me. He didn't even look at me, only went down the stairs, grabbed a surfboard and took off toward the beach. The man was vaguely familiar, but it seemed lots of men his age were taking up surfing these days.

I stood, glancing back and forth between the beach and the doorway, not knowing whether to go in.

"Hello," I called, peering around the door frame and into the hall. No one was around that I could see, so I walked in and closed the door behind me.

Beyond the vestibule was the living room. A large blue patterned couch sat before a wall of floor-to-ceiling windows that overlooked the beach. I caught a glimpse of the man who passed me paddling out into the ocean. Quickly, I drew my gaze away from him and back to the room. There was a gorgeous blue rug over bleached wooden floors. Dark beams lined the ceiling and added a nice accent to the white-washed walls. I decided the interior of Mrs. North's home was quite the opposite of its exterior.

With not a soul in sight, I wandered around the first floor. The dining area gave a warm welcome with its red and black braided rug and mismatched painted chairs that varied in height and put me in mind of Snow White and the Seven Dwarfs. In fact, there were exactly seven chairs.

Past the dining room was the kitchen, and it was stunning like something from a home decorating channel. It was there, as I admired the eight-burner range, that I met the infamous Mrs. North.

"Made yourself right at home, I see," she said, taking a drag off what I can only describe as being a candy cane cigarette. With each puff, the room filled with the aroma of mint. "Good, I like a gal who gets the lay of the land before taking on a mission."

"I'm so, so sorry. I... I tried to knock, and, well, you see there was this man, and..." I could feel my face flush. Perspiration formed under my arms and on the back of my neck. This was not a good start.

"You would mean my husband. He's off limits to you, by the way," she said, and with a nod of her head beckoned me to follow her to the living room.

So, she did know me. Must have seen the publicity, the photos, and the articles. Lady M and Felix and I were quite a juicy story for months. It's true, he was her husband first, but, in my defense, Lady M had dumped him. I was going through my own break-up, and what had begun as a rebound ended in marriage. Still, Lady M kept her hooks in Felix. He couldn't or wouldn't shake free from her. Our musical chair marriages were the talk of the Broadway community. We were every gossip columnist's dream.

"I can explain about all of that," I said, settling into an overstuffed blue denim chair where I immediately sank, leaving my feet dangling as if I was a small child.

"Please," said Mrs. North. "I don't want you to ruin the story for me. It certainly kept me entertained during the long travels with my husband. Usually, reading while in a moving vehicle leaves me nauseous. Nico is an absolute horrid driver under the best of circumstances, but even his erratic driving could not keep me from the paper and the saga of you and Ma..."

I held up my hand. "I can't bear to have her name mentioned, so if you wouldn't mind, I'd rather you not use it."

"Oh, darling, I perfectly understand. The woman is a dragon. Tea?" she asked, ringing a small crystal bell and lighting up another candy cane. "I'll have Holly bring it in."

A woman about the size of Mrs. Doolittle, barely four feet high, entered the room with a tray holding a teapot, two porcelain cups with matching saucers, a pitcher that presumably held cream, and a bowl with brown sugar cubes spilling from the top. Without a word she placed the tray on a large, tufted ottoman then left without as much as raising her eyes to us.

"The job is quite simple," began Mrs. North after we prepared and sipped our tea. "I tell you what I need, and you do it." She smiled tightly. Mrs. North was both exactly what I imagined and very different than I expected. She was at least six feet tall and slender, with sculpted cheekbones like a model. Her hair was silver white, cut into a short bob. She shimmered like sun on a lake. I was self-conscious of my own looks and felt rather drab next to her.

"I'm not much of a typist," I said, and this made her laugh. It was a sound that instantly made me feel happy.

"Darling, no typing is required."

"But what about your responses to the letters you receive?" I asked.

"Letters? My husband's team answers those," she said, scrunching her face into a quizzical expression. "Oh! You mean the advice column? Yes, I see. Those I just read into the microphone and send it to the newspaper. Someone in their office types it up. No, your job will be keeping my events straight, organizing my calendar, those sorts of things."

I could do that, I kept repeating to myself. Despite our personal lives, I had been an exceptional assistant to Lady M. Organizing was one of my strongest skills.

"Now that's all settled, let me show you to your accommodations." Mrs. North stood and seemed taller than earlier. She brushed down the front of her white sweater and light gray linen pants. Those two pieces of clothing looked as if they cost the same as my entire wardrobe.

"Hold on. My accommodations?"

"Yes, darling. You will be living here. I need an assistant I can call at any moment."

"B-b-but I have a home with Mrs. Doolittle." I was ashamed to hear the crack in my voice and hoped she didn't notice the tears I could feel forming in my eyes. I wasn't ready to leave Mrs. Doolittle, not yet. Maybe not ever. I was more at home in the boarding house than I'd been as a child with my own parents, now so many years ago. I closed my eyes, hoping to ward off the feeling of panic growing inside me. This was too much of a change.

Mrs. North sighed deeply, looked up at the ceiling then back at me before sitting in the chair. "Natalie, I understand you've been through quite the troublesome time, not only with your previous job and marriages, but with your parents. I'm sure you've created a cozy nest for yourself at the Doolittle's, but I assure you, you will be comfortable here. I promise, and it's one of my jobs to keep promises." She watched me for a second. "You are ready, aren't you?"

I looked into Mrs. North's eyes and a calmness came over me. Though I still had my doubts, I thought of how encouraging Mrs. Doolittle had been that morning. I couldn't let her down.

I nodded then followed Mrs. North up the stairs.

When she opened the door at the end of the hall, inside was the room of my childhood dreams. Cream-colored walls were decorated with paintings of pink and lavender flowers. A queen-sized four poster bed stood at the center facing windows that overlooked the ocean. This was the exact room I had cut from a magazine when I was about eight years old and had enclosed it in a letter to Santa. It was the only thing I'd asked for that year. I didn't get the room of my dreams; however, I did get an additional bedroom when my parents divorced early the next year. Neither room was magazine worthy.

"This is... amazing. It's beautiful, and perfect, but I just don't know. I wasn't planning on taking another job like this," I said. My gaze kept falling to the ocean and I imagined laying in the bed with the sound of the waves crashing and lulling me to sleep.

"I am an excellent judge of character, Natalie, and you can trust me when I say you were born for this job. Shall I send for your things?" Mrs. North asked, then shook her head. "No, that won't do, will it?" She smiled and her face softened. "I'll tell you what, you go back to Mrs. Doolittle and say your goodbyes. I'll expect you in the morning, nine o'clock sharp. You'll find I don't like to be kept waiting."

"Mrs. Doolittle said this was just a temporary position, but it feels like you're telling me this is a permanent arrangement." The ocean suddenly seemed dangerous rather than comforting.

"Everything is permanent, and nothing stays the same," replied Mrs. North before leaving the room.

"What does that mean?" I asked, but when I walked into the hallway she was gone. Only the scent of peppermint lingered.

Mrs. Doolittle was in the kitchen when I returned, her hands in a huge bowl of dough. I'd spent some time walking along the boardwalk, thinking about Mrs. North, her odd house, the beautiful bedroom, and all the uncertainty I felt. I was sure that in agreeing to this job I'd be giving up a lot of my freedom. I was nearly fifty years old and had spent most of my life following the directions of other people, first my parents, then my husband and Lady

M. These last few years had given me space I hadn't even realized I needed.

"Tell me everything," said Mrs. Doolittle when she saw me watching her. "What was she like? Is the house creepy? It looks like it would be. Will you be working at the newspaper with her?" She wiped her hands on a cloth and sat across the table from me.

"Mrs. North smokes odd striped cigarettes," I said, realizing that was the only thing I could remember about the woman. "And she wants me to live there with her in th-that house." Before I could get the words out, I was crying, sobbing actually. I was not one for tears. I didn't cry when my husband left me—either time—or when I lost my job, or even when my father died. However, the thought of leaving Mrs. Doolittle, the place I was most at home, the place where I'd become a better version of me, was crushing.

"Oh dearie, come now. You should be happy. This is a wonderful opportunity. Why, here's your chance to prove how everyone was wrong about you. You can show them how good you are at your job, and that your main goal wasn't looking for a rich husband. Say, is there a Mr. North? Best to stay clear of him. Just saying, dearie." Mrs. Doolittle handed me her dish towel to wipe my face. "I'm not going anywhere, and your room and job will be waiting for you when you get back."

This made me cry harder. "That's the thing. I don't think I'm coming back. She intends to keep me. Forever." I blew my nose in the terry cloth. "Mrs. North said that everything is permanent, and nothing stays the same. I don't know what that means, but I was instructed to collect my things, tell you goodbye, and be back by nine o'clock in the morning."

Mrs. Doolittle sat back against the chair. "Natalie, we will see each other. You're upset over nothing. She's not going to hold you captive, I'm sure." She giggled.

I wasn't so sure. There was indeed something very odd about the house and Mrs. North. If only I could remember her face. Everything else was so clear to me—the room, the girl who served tea, even her husband grabbing his surfboard.

"I'm not going," I finally said. "I'm sorry if this disappoints you, really, I am. You've been nothing but kind to me and I don't want to bring a bad review to your business, but I just can't do it." I dashed from the table and up to my room, slamming the door behind me.

All that crying had left me exhausted and soon I fell into a deep sleep. I dreamed Mrs. North was in my room sitting on the side of my bed. She was dressed in a red suit trimmed in white fur and smoking one of her candy canes.

"I understand your concern," she said, a great plume of smoke flowing from her nostrils like she was a dragon. "You will be fine, I assure you. I've been waiting until the time was right to call you."

"Call me?" I asked, sitting up in bed.

"Yes. Do you know your letter was the first I ever received? It's how I came to write the advice column. I knew then there would come a time you and I would work together. I need you, Natalie. Don't disappoint me."

An hour later, I woke up. My room was dark, but the air was filled with the fragrance of peppermint.

Chapter 2

"Quitting is always an option," Mrs. Doolittle said, as she walked me down the long, picture-filled hallway to the front door the next morning.

It's funny to say with two divorces behind me, but I'd never quit anything in my life. He had quit me. Well, maybe I'd put him in the position where he had no other choice but to quit me.

I smiled and thanked Mrs. Doolittle again for her kindness and patience, but I was determined not to look back as I crossed the street and headed for the bridge. As I walked over Silver Lake, I thought of that saying about crossing bridges. At least I hadn't burned this one down.

The house stood quiet, watching as if it were waiting for me. I started up the steps and once again met Mr. North coming out the door. He was in his wetsuit, his long white hair pulled back into a ponytail. I noticed a tattoo of a holly leaf on the side of his neck. His skin was tan, but it seemed more from wind burn than the sun. He turned to me and smiled, revealing the whitest teeth I'd ever seen.

"Good morning," he called out. "Welcome to North Pole Beach."

"North Pole Beach?" I set my suitcase and box down.

Mr. North walked over to the surfboard leaning against the garage. "What can I say? My two favorite things are Christmas and the beach."

"Oh, I get it. The house's name, am I right?" I smiled.

He smiled back, his face appearing younger than his gray hair and beard led me to believe. "That's it."

I looked quickly away. This is how it had started with Felix. Would I ever learn?

"I better get in. Don't want to be late for my first day." I grabbed my belongings and scurried up the stairs.

Mrs. North stood at the door watching. "He's too friendly, that one," she said as I entered.

"Nice man," I muttered as I passed her, making my way through the living room to the stairs and to my new room.

I turned. Mrs. North was directly behind me. I hadn't even heard her footsteps. The carpeting must be extra plush.

"Here." Mrs. North handed me a sheet of paper. It resembled a scroll, the kind you see in movies with kings and queens. "I'd like you to start at number one and work your way down the list, but, if need be, do them in the order that you're able. The important thing is to complete the list by noon. I'll have another for you after lunch." She turned to go, then stopped. "By the way, you'll find your lunch in the kitchen at exactly twelve-thirty."

Before I could respond, she was gone. The list had twenty-two items, which seemed a lot to do in less than four hours considering I'd have to figure out where things were kept. Number one on the list was to organize the letters she'd received into piles—love, family, and money, in that order.

The house was as quiet as it had been the day before. I went to the kitchen where I found the lady who had served us tea. "Good morning," I said. She nodded in response but said nothing. "Could you please tell me where Mrs. North keeps the letters she receives?"

"Which ones? Her personal correspondence or the ones she answers for the paper?"

"Does she read her mail in separate places?" I asked.

"No." The woman looked at me if I was odd. "She reads them all in the sitting room. It's the replies she separates."

"And where would I find any of this correspondence?"

"Why, in her office, of course. It's the red door behind the stairs. The cherry red, not the tomato red. That door belongs to Mr. C. He doesn't like to be disturbed after he comes back from his swim."

I nodded my thanks, wondering who Mr. C was, and headed back out through the living room and around the staircase where I found two red doors just as she said, though I couldn't have told you which was tomato and which was cherry.

Mrs. North came out of the one on the left as I stood there. "Ah, good, there you are. Come in. Here's a desk for you." She motioned to a small table that was polished to a shine. I noticed the wood was cherry, as was the large desk and the bookshelves.

Maybe Mrs. North's red was cherry. "If you'd be more comfortable, I can have this placed in your room."

"No, right here is fine," I said, taking note of the fax machine and a mimeograph. The last one of those I'd seen was in the office of my high school. I hoped Mrs. North didn't expect me to know how that worked.

"Good. I'll let you have at it. I'm meeting Nico for a smoothie." Mrs. North made a sour face. "It seems surfing and smoothies go together for Nico. My idea of a smoothie is a frozen Brandy Alexander. It must be five o'clock somewhere, right, darling?" She waved then was gone.

There were eight tightly packed mail bags. I couldn't even lift them, so I pushed one over and made myself comfortable on the floor. At first it was odd reading the letters people wrote. It felt wrong, like I was spying. Mrs. North was right, the letters all fit into one of the categories she had mentioned. Some could have gone under all three.

As I made my way through one bag then another, I remembered the dream I had of Mrs. North the night before. *"Your letter was the first I ever received,"* she had said. I was positive, even during my troubles with my parents, my marriage, and work, I'd never written to anyone for advice, let alone Mrs. North. It was just a silly dream.

I surprised myself by not only accomplishing every item on the list but completing thirty minutes before lunch time. After tidying up my workspace, I took a walk in the yard. Mr. North's surfboard lay in the grass next to the house. It was heavier than I realized, as I struggled to put it up against the wall. I smoothed my hands down the board. It was a good one, not like those I'd seen in the shops in town. He'd probably had it custom made.

Keeping an eye on the time, I strolled the garden. It was pleasant with the fragrance of the last roses mixed with the salt air. I'd taken the final turn and was headed to the kitchen door when I heard voices. Ducking back under the arbor, I spied Holly and a man who appeared to be the mail carrier.

"Getting ready for one of his jaunts, I imagine," she was saying, as he handed her a small parcel wrapped in brown paper. "The missus is never quite herself when he's away, especially near the holidays. Who knows where he's off to." Holly shook her head.

From where I stood, hidden to be truthful, I couldn't hear his response, but from the way Holly moved, I could swear she was flirting.

Once he walked away, I headed straight for the kitchen where my lunch of an egg salad sandwich on toast and slices of tomato and pickles were left on a tray at the counter. Holly never came inside. I sat alone and ate trying not to think of what Mrs. Doolittle was serving at home.

Good to her word, a new list was at my desk after lunch. Mrs. North was absent, and the house still. I was sure I was the only person here. As much as I was tempted to explore while alone, I pushed curiosity aside and concentrated on the work left to me. In the evening, I once again ate from a tray on my own in the kitchen.

I missed Mrs. Doolittle terribly, even her annoying habits like listening in on phone calls, the clicking of her heels on the hardwood floor at all hours, and hiding the television remote so we were stuck watching endless episodes of *ER*, the George Clooney years. It was nice to have someone to talk to at meals and to listen to the other ladies talk about their day at work, even what's-her-name.

Sleep came over me quickly, though I hadn't felt the least bit tired.

Mrs. North was once again perched at the end of my bed. "Darling, is this an inconvenient time?"

"What?" I asked, rubbing my eyes.

"I work better at night, under the cloak of darkness," she said and grinned. "You've done excellent work. Too bad for you, however. It will only encourage me to give you more."

I think she was still talking when I drifted back to sleep. In the morning though, I noticed my bedroom door was locked from the inside. I really hoped I wouldn't be dreaming of her every night.

The next few days passed much like the first: quiet house, meals on trays, jobs listed on crisp white pages, and dreams of Mrs. North. Organizing the letters for her advice column was interesting and I tried to guess who in the tiny beach towns might have written them. Each ended with a clever sign off: "Dazed in Dewey," "Loveless in Lewes," "Betrothed in Bethany," "Fearful in Fenwick," all awaiting the practical advice of Mrs. North. Maybe I needed to write one. I'd call myself "Silenced in Silver Lake."

When the office work was completed, I spent the rest of my days running errands, from picking up her dry cleaning to buying pomegranates at Fresh Market. There were also her radio interviews to schedule. Mrs. North never made public appearances.

I was pleasantly surprised to find Holly at the kitchen table with her dinner when I arrived. Without asking, I slid my plate of salad and my bowl of mushroom stew off the tray and onto the table across from her. "It's really nice to have company at dinner. I feel we haven't had much of a chance to talk or even officially meet," I said.

"Normally I eat with Mr. and Mrs. Cl... I mean, Mrs. North. Tonight they, she's, they're planning something in the garage." Holly focused on her stew as she spoke. "They like to plan for the holidays and they're a bit behind schedule with, you know, stuff going on."

"What would that be?" I asked sipping at my stew. Things stayed hot here, not like Mrs. Doolittle's lukewarm soup and blackened biscuits. How I missed that woman.

"Nothing. Never mind me," Holly said before clearing her place and scampering out the back door. Another dinner alone.

Mrs. North stood silently beside my bed. At first, I thought it was one of my weird dreams I'd been having since I met her.

"I must speak to you immediately, Natalie. Please meet me in my office."

I sat up slowly, watching her go, her long silver-gray dressing gown flying out behind her. The clock read 3:00 A.M. She wasn't kidding when she said I was to be available at all hours.

Wrapping a flannel blanket around my shoulders, I pushed my feet into a pair of wooly slippers, then shuffled from the bedroom and down to her office wondering if I should have brushed my teeth first. Note to self: keep mouthwash on nightstand in case of impromptu late-night meetings.

Her red door was propped open, looking more like blood than cherry in the moonlight. I tapped gently before going in. Mrs. North sat behind her wide, carved cherry desk, her hands covering her face. A large, star-shaped diamond glittered from her finger. *North Star*, I thought.

"Mrs. North, are you well? Can I get you something?" Was she crying? It seemed impossible to think. Lady M often ended her evenings by dissolving in tears, but this was not expected from the ever-cool Mrs. North.

With her face still covered, Mrs. North said, "I have no other options than to take you into my confidence."

I hoped with everything in me that this upset did not involve her husband, or any man for that matter. "It's the oath all personal assistants take. Anything told to us in confidence by our employers must be taken to the grave. My lips are sealed, I'm like a priest." A tinkle of laughter escaped me.

Mrs. North's hands dropped heavily on to her desk, the ring on her finger clinking as it hit. Her eyes were dry, and her mouth was pressed into a thin line. There was no hint of a smile.

I slunk into a chair. "What is it? What's wrong?" I saw terror in her eyes and my heartbeat quickened. I tried to imagine what terrible thing had occurred since we'd gone to bed. Anything this serious should maybe be discussed with her husband and not an assistant who had worked for her mere days. I once again cringed at the thought the problem might be him.

"Is it to do with the letters? Is someone threatening you? Has someone revealed a murderous plot?" I asked.

"Murderous plots? Good grief, darling. How your imagination does run wild. No, it's none of those things. Nothing at all to do with the column or the paper. It has to do with Nico, my husband."

Great. I just knew this kind of agony would be about some man. Mine always were. "Is he cheating on you?" I asked. I thought back to what I'd overheard in the garden. Apparently, Mr. North, Nico, always disappeared for a time between Thanksgiving and Christmas. Maybe he was keeping another family, a secret life.

"He's not cheating, and he has no secret life or other family. If only it were that simple," answered Mrs. North.

Had I said that out loud about the family and life? "No, of course not. But what has he done?"

"He's done nothing wrong. It was me. I took something from his office, was most careless with it and it's now missing, fallen into the wrong hands." Mrs. North wrung her own hands as she said the words. "This was stuck to a package Holly received." She pushed a scrap of paper over to me.

My hand shook as I reached for it. *"My mission has been compromised. I'm afraid they know my true identity,"* was scrawled in black ink across a torn piece of butcher's paper.

"What does this mean?" I asked.

Mrs. North studied the magnificent ring then folded both hands together before answering. "I'm sure this message came from Ivy, my assistant... my *other* personal assistant." Her voice was soft, nearly a whisper. "I sent her to work undercover for the people who stole what rightfully belongs to Nico. Unfortunately, it seems that not only has she been unable to retrieve what was stolen, but maybe she is now in danger."

"What was stolen and who took it? Shouldn't the police be involved, or at least Nico? I mean Mr. North?" I said, nearly hiccupping in panic. What kind of people was I working for?

"Nico must not know. He's depressed enough with the way of the world as it is, and this, this I believe would cause him to completely give up and want to surf full-time." Mrs. North came from behind her desk and sat in the chair next to mine. "The police would never understand. Even you will find it hard to believe once I tell you what we are searching for."

"Mrs. North, I can see how truly afraid you are. I'll believe whatever it is you tell me, and you can trust that what you say will go no further than this room." It was true, I could keep a secret, even a secret that would have won me back my husband. But I was Lady M's confidante, and it was a big part of my job to not reveal the things I'd seen and heard.

"I realize most people believe this to be a story, a legend, much like Excalibur, but I assure you what I say is the absolute truth. The thing that was stolen from me was... the Naughty and Nice list."

I was sitting literally at the edge of my seat at this point, and the tension in the room was like a bomb might go off at any minute. "The Naughty and Nice List?" I exploded with laughter. Who could have ever guessed Mrs. North to be such a practical joker? This must be some sort of hazing because I was the newest employee.

"Please, Natalie, keep your voice down," said Mrs. North, as she rushed over and shut the door. "It's important that Nico never discover the list is missing. You don't know what we've been through over the years. The wars and plagues, the inhumanity toward certain people and groups, the hunger and famine and desperation of so many. Those things we got through, we were there to help as were others, but lately..." Mrs. North flopped into the chair, causing it to tip back only slightly, but enough to alarm me.

My laughter was now hard in my throat. Mrs. North no longer seemed sleek and sophisticated, but tired and alone. "I don't fully understand what you're telling me," I said, and reached for her hand so she'd have an anchor, someone steady to hold on to.

"I'm telling you what I tell very few people, for who honestly would believe me?" She seemed to search my face for some sign of understanding. She must have found it for she continued. "You see, though my maiden name is North, I am Mrs. Nicholas Claus."

I pulled back my hand and rubbed my arms to reassure myself that I was indeed awake and that this wasn't another Mrs. North dream. Was this woman, my employer, seriously telling me her husband was Santa Claus? "Maybe you just need a warm drink. Milk, perhaps?" I scuttled off to the kitchen before she had a chance to reply.

I brought us each a cup of tea—peppermint, of course. We sat in silence sipping from our mugs, not looking at each other. Did Mrs. North spend too much time alone in her house? Had her husband's obsession with all things Christmas led her into a world where she now believed she was actually living in the North Pole? Maybe he believed this as well. I started to think a doctor was needed more than the police.

"I'm not living in a make-believe world, Natalie, and I don't need a doctor. I'm quite sane, thank you."

The sound of her voice caused me to jump. We'd been quiet for so long. "How do you always seem to know what I'm thinking?"

"It's both a blessing and a curse," Mrs. North answered. "Nico is much more perceptive than I am. He also knows when you are sleeping and when you are awake." She said this with a straight face. "It's true."

I set my cup carefully on the desk blotter. "Mrs. North," I began than remembered something about not disagreeing with someone's delusion. "I mean, Mrs. Claus. Don't you think it would be best if we did call your doctor? Maybe you've had an injury. Have you fallen recently? Perhaps you've hit your head. I was in a car accident a few years back and couldn't write my name for nearly a month. Concussion," I said, pointing my finger to the back of my head.

"That was not long after your first wedding, I remember," said Mrs. North.

"Okay, now... how would you know that? My own mother doesn't know that."

"Natalie, I told you when I came to see you at Mrs. Doolittle's. I've been keeping an eye on you." Mrs. North put her cup down, too. "I meant what I said. It was because of your letter that I began writing the advice column."

"What letter?" I asked.

Mrs. North stood, went round the desk and opened the top drawer. She removed a yellowed envelope and handed it to me. It was addressed to Ms. Claus. I recognized my childish handwriting immediately. I'd had trouble with cursive and my R's always turned to S's.

"Go ahead, open it." She gave me a timid smile.

The paper was soft, like it had been handled many times. Tears came to my eyes as I read.

Dear Ms. Claus,

I have been a good girl most days. I try to stay quiet and out of Mommy and Daddy's way. I don't want any toys this year. I have too many, Mommy says. I only want a nice room where I can stay. I promise to keep it clean. I sent you a picture of it.

Thank you,
Natalie

P.S. Can you tell me what to do so Mommy and Daddy will be happy again?

Inside the envelope was the picture I'd clipped out of the magazine. It was identical to the room upstairs.

"You see, darling, every child writes to Santa, but no one ever remembers me. When that letter came with my name on it, I was extremely flattered. I hung on to it, as you can tell, and tried to answer you, but Nico said that might confuse things a bit. I believe he gave you a beautiful doll with a cradle that year. It was really the best we could do. You understand, don't you?"

"I don't understand any of this. I mean, why are you here? Aren't Santa and Mrs. Claus supposed to be at the North Pole, you know, with snow, and elves, and talking reindeer?"

"Reindeer do not talk, Natalie. That's just made up for television," she said and shook her head. "As I've told you, we've been through a lot. Fewer young men and women want to stay at the workshop. Over the years, we went from a toy factory of more than two thousand employees down to just twenty workers. Remaining in the same business as your family has gone out of fashion in the past few generations. Elves these days don't stay. They go to college and explore the world, which I think is wonderful, but they never come back. They forget, and as time passes, their memories of the castle, the workshop, and the North Pole disappear."

I sat up straight. "Mrs. Doolittle?" Her tiny stature was so similar to Holly's.

"Ah, yes, our Violet. Went off on holiday, met a man, married him, never returned. Lovely girl, she was." Mrs. North touched my shoulder. "Natalie, I know this seems fantastical, but it's real. I'm real, and I'm dealing with a man, my husband, who is losing his sense of purpose."

"How can Santa lose his purpose?" I hardly believed the words coming out of my mouth. "He has a definite job every year, doesn't he?"

"He did, but that's before The Everywhere Corporation began taking over. Fewer children write these days to my husband. Why bother when with a click of the keyboard you can order anything and have it delivered to your door?

The children of today do not want to wait. They've been raised by parents who have little free time and have grown accustomed to shopping online." Mrs. North stared at her own outdated laptop on the desk.

"Santa is Santa. No huge company can take his place," I said.

"Can't they?" Mrs. North slumped wearily in her chair. "Think back to your own childhood, or even when you were in your early twenties. Do you remember the coziness of the bookstores, just going in to see what was new? Think of all the things that drew you in, the weight of books in your hand, the smooth feel of the pages, the fragrance of the coffee brewing and the books combined to give you a sense of all the possibilities the shop held."

I closed my eyes and conjured up Browse About Books, which still held all those wonderful feelings for me, but I knew she was right. Many bookstores had closed because it was easier to order from home than to drive someplace.

"Online shopping has taken the place of experiences. We've all let convenience numb our senses. Soon Christmas will fall in the same way."

"That can't happen. I mean, kids wait for Christmas. They still write letters and leave out cookies, right?"

Mrs. North shook her head. "Things began to slide when every department store hired a Santa."

"That was years ago," I said.

"Every demise begins somewhere. Nico thought it fun, even encouraged it. You know that old fool once slipped in as a replacement for the Macy's Santa during one parade? He thought of it as an honor, but I could see what was happening. Before long, letters that would have come to him began being left with the mall Santas or some fancy mailbox the store rigged up. It's true, we still received a great many, but the numbers declined with each passing year. Last year he received only four hundred and twenty-eight. Do you know how many children are in this world?"

"So, who is on this missing list then?" I asked.

"Those who continue to believe. Not all on the list have the ability to write, but their intentions, their hopes and dreams are known to us. As long as Nico has the list, it keeps his belief from flickering. You see, he needs the spirit of Christmas as much as the world needs him."

"But what good does the list do for The Everywhere Corporation?" I wanted to know.

"As far as I can figure, two things. First it gives them the names of children they can advertise to, children they may not have access to or have known about otherwise. Secondly, with Santa out of the way, Christmas can come every day. Why wait a year for that bike when you can get it tomorrow with free shipping? Many parents are already on board with celebrating every single event in their children's lives. This company wants to take advantage of that."

I remembered how holidays were before my parents split up. Christmas could only begin after the Thanksgiving meal had been cleaned up and we watched *Miracle on 34th Street* on television. The next morning, Mom would take me on the bus to go downtown to watch the unveiling of the decorated windows of Hutzler's and Stewart's department stores. I always watched Santa from afar, too afraid to sit on his lap. Now, in this room, even over forty years later, I could feel the coolness of the air on my cheeks, the smell of the popcorn the stores had handed out, and the touch of my mother's gloved hand in mine. These were memories of experiences that children sitting in front of computer screens would never know.

"Do you know for sure The Everywhere Corporation has the Naughty and Nice list? How would they have access to it?" I asked.

"I'm positive." Mrs. North went to the bookshelf and opened a copy of Dickens's *A Christmas Carol.* "This came the day I realized the list was missing from my desk."

She handed me a Christmas card. The front cover pictured a Santa smoking a pipe while stuffing a stocking. Inside it read, *"Hope Santa enjoys his retirement."* It seemed rather threatening to me. I handed the card back over.

"You see, the higher ups at The Everywhere Corporation have reached out to Nico on several occasions asking to go into business with him. They wanted to buy the castle and the workshop in the North Pole. Silly men. No one who wasn't born there could ever live in those weather conditions. They tried to send someone in to organize a union with the elves, unaware they already had one and that everyone was being paid well with outstanding benefits. They simply could not buy us out or get what they wanted. Instead, now they are hitting below the belt, so to speak. They seem to know Nico is a bit down in the mouth, so they're going for that angle. Kicking him while he's low."

"Obviously, this is an inside job. Someone here must have taken the list and given or sold it to them," I said.

"There are very few people who work here for us, and even fewer who know our true identities. I don't see how that could be," answered Mrs. North.

"How else would they have access to your office, to your house?"

Mrs. North rested her chin on her hand. "I know what you say must be true, but I have a difficult time believing Ivy, Holly, or Paulo would conspire against us."

"Who's Paulo?" The only man I'd seen around here was Nico, other than the mailman.

"Paulo helps Nico with the yard and builds surfboards. He's usually here quite often, but I can't say I've seen much of him in the last week."

"I'm listing him as suspect number one," I said snatching a pad of paper and pen from Mrs. North's desk. "Now, Ivy is the other personal assistant, right?" I wrote her name down. "Holly is the lady who makes meals and such. Does she know about, well, your real names?"

"Nico and Beira are our real names. Nico calls me Bee, though." Mrs. North blushed when she said this. "Both Holly and Ivy know exactly who we are. They're sisters and moved here with us. Paulo doesn't, as far as I know. Nico met him here at the beach. He also has never been inside the house. He and Nico work in the garage or the shed."

"What about Holly? Could she maybe have a crush on Paulo? Would she have given him the list? Perhaps they are working together."

"I can't imagine that. Holly is quiet and keeps to herself. You make many good points, though." Mrs.

North smiled at me, her face more relaxed than I'd seen since I moved here.

"So, how are we going to get this list back and rescue Ivy in the process?" I asked.

Mrs. North winked at me. "I've an idea. You're not going to like it at all."

Chapter 3

The Everywhere Corporation was housed in a large warehouse that, from the faded signage near the gate, had once been a sail manufacturer. Mrs. North and I puttered along Route 1 for several miles out of Rehoboth in her dusty 1962 blue and white Mk1 Cortina.

"Are you sure this is a good idea?" I asked, opening my window to release some of the peppermint smoke. "What if you're recognized? What if we can't find Ivy? This is a bad idea. I'm not comfortable at all."

Mrs. North tapped her lit candy cane out her window. "Darling, as I've explained before, no one knows me. You yourself admitted after our first meeting you had no recollection of what I looked like. When society visualizes Mrs. Claus they see her as an elderly, plump woman with snow-white hair, rosy cheeks, and twinkling blue eyes. Would you say that describes me?"

"Well, no. Why is that the image we have of Mrs. Claus?"

"It's all about marketing. Nico and I enjoy our quiet life. We come and go as we please with no one recognizing us. That's the way we like it. We concocted the image of the jolly old elf years ago.

Actually, we got the idea from that Clement Clarke Moore fellow. Lovely story, that was."

"You're right to say no one would confuse your Nico with Santa Claus. He's much too fit." A brief image of Nico in his tight wetsuit crossed my mind. I smacked my forehead. What was wrong with me? Who has fantasies about Santa, for goodness sake! *I'm definitely going to end up on the Naughty list if we ever get it back.*

Then it occurred to me, I might already be there.

"Are you alright?" Mrs. North asked frowning at me. "We should be at the front entrance in a few minutes, so pull yourself together."

Gravel spattered against the car as we pulled under the archway that displayed "Everywhere" in large red letters on a blue canvas banner.

My stomach nearly dropped to my knees as I stepped from the car. I tugged at the lanyard hanging from my neck that identified me as Kristina Kelly, assistant manager. Glancing in the side car mirror, I barely recognized myself behind cat's eyeglasses, with blue eye shadow, and the heavily teased and sprayed hairdo Mrs. North had insisted upon. *"We must look professional,"* she had said. Instead, I could pass for an extra on *Mad Men.*

"Here we go, Nat... I mean Kristina. Look lively and follow my lead." Mrs. North, herself dressed as if she just escaped from a 1950's sitcom, strode ahead of me up the ramp, and heaved open the glass-plated door.

Inside, the space was sparse and ultra-modern with shiny chrome and glass tables, smooth gray leather chairs, dangling lightbulbs in cages, surrounded by concrete walls and galvanized steel pipes. Mrs. North nodded approvingly at the setup. I knew from the many books on her shelves that she admired modern design.

"May I help you?" asked the woman behind the desk. She was nearly as tall as Mrs. North and as sleek as the office around her. She flicked her long blonde hair off her shoulder to reveal her name tag. "Gazelle" was printed in fine black letters. The name certainly suited her.

"Yes, good morning. I am Hedda Nelson, and this is Kristina Kelly. We are here from the Safety and Health of Workers Organization." She pulled a clipboard from her satchel. "We have you scheduled to be inspected and evaluated today."

Gazelle checked her computer screen. "Ah yes, I see it here. We have reserved Conference Room B for your interviews. Mr. Edgemere will show you around. Let me buzz him. You both can take a seat over there. Would you like coffee, tea, or freshly squeezed juice while you wait?"

"Nothing for me," I said, my voice dry and croaking.

"No, thank you, darling," said Mrs. North.

We sat on stiff chairs, not at all the soft leather I'd expected, for only a few minutes before Mr. Edgemere appeared. Now we had a problem.

I knew him as Mr. Caramel Corn. He liked the kind with Old Bay and was a frequent customer at Dolle's. That's the thing with working for a temporary agency, you meet so many more people than you would in a steady job.

I dropped my glance to my hands and whispered, “He’s a customer at the candy shop. He may remember me.”

Mrs. North stood and pulled me up by my elbow. “Hold your head high, darling, and smile. He won’t recognize you. We are both at the age of invisibility.” She stepped toward him, her hand outstretched. “You must be Mr. Edgemere. I am Mrs. Nelson, and this is my associate Mrs. Kelly. We are here to oversee your inspection.”

Mr. Edgemere wiped his hand over the top of his balding head and stared at us from watery blue eyes before shaking her hand. His red nose indicated he was suffering from a cold or allergies. I discreetly passed Mrs. North a disinfectant wipe when he released her hand. Being only several weeks away from Christmas, I couldn’t let her get sick this close to the busiest time on her calendar.

If Mr. Edgemere recognized me, he showed no indication of it. We followed him through the main lobby, past four or five glass-enclosed offices, and up a wide staircase to the main packing room.

I noticed two things on our walk; first, the glass offices all held the most beautiful and young people who worked here, and secondly, if Ivy was being kept hostage, I could see no places to hide.

“In this area we have our packing stations,” Mr. Edgemere said, the thin hairs of his mustache quivering as he spoke. “The orders are printed out and packed by our staff. We’ve always had a five-star rating from our customers. A minimal number of items are returned, and not one of those because they are broken. Each order is handled with the upmost care. We..." A loud crash drowned out the rest of his sentence.

Mrs. North and I turned to see a woman about my age scurrying around a table to retrieve merchandise from the floor. She picked up two boxes containing a toaster and a blender, and had shoved them into a larger box by the time we reached her.

"That's four this week, Maggie," Mr. Edgemere said, emphasizing each word. "This is your second warning."

"Sorry, Mr. Edgemere," Maggie said. I noticed then that one of her arms was in a cast.

"What happened there?" I asked, pointing to her injury.

"Oh, it's nothing, really. I took a tumble carrying laundry down my basement steps," she said, keeping her gaze on the box she was taping.

"When did this happen?" Mrs. North wanted to know.

"A few days ago, but I'm fine enough now," Maggie said, giving a slight laugh.

"Yes, our Mary's been with us for a few years. Since we opened, in fact." Mr. Edgemere's smile looked more like a grimace to me.

"You mean Maggie," I said, not hiding the contempt that was building inside of me for Mr. Caramel Corn.

"Yes, of course, Maggie. I did mean Maggie." At least he had the decency to blush with embarrassment.

"Very well, then," said Mrs. North. "You, darling, shall be the first person we interview."

Mr. Edgemere didn't even pretend to smile now. "Interview? I knew you were to speak to a few team members, but I really can't have this crew away from their stations. We have a schedule, you know, a deadline to meet, and a quota to fulfill. Really, I must ask you to limit your interviews to the members of our front office."

Mrs. North pulled herself up to her full height, which was a good six inches above Mr. Edgemere. "I conduct the interviews as I see fit. A few of your team members, as you call them, will be interviewed along with the crew. We will stroll around each floor and then have a sit-down with the employees we choose to see. I am told we have a room available. We'll begin in forty-five minutes."

I said nothing, only nodded in response to Mrs. North's words. Mr. Edgemere's face turned faintly pink, then rapidly became purple. You could see by the puckering of his lips and the bulging vein pulsing near his jaw that he wanted to say more, but was holding it in.

Mrs. North paid him no attention, just turned on her heel and made her way back down the corridor.

We were made comfortable in one of the glass offices. Mrs. North sent Mr. Edgemere for coffee as if he were an intern. We could still hear him muttering long after we'd lost sight of him.

"While we have a moment," said Mrs. North, leaning toward me, "let me tell you how this will work. I will stay here and ask a few questions of the employees. You, on the premise of fetching the next person to be interviewed, will search for Ivy in all the spaces we cannot see. She must be here someplace."

"But suppose she's not. Someone could have taken her to another location. Or it could be worse. Maybe she's..." I bit my lip. Though I didn't want to think of the many fates that could have befallen Ivy, it was something we needed to consider.

"Really, Natalie. You must stop watching and reading all those crime dramas."

"How do you know what... oh, right. No matter what I'm reading, we have to face the fact that she could be in real danger."

"I highly doubt that," said Mrs. North, but she quickly looked away, and in that movement, I knew she was just as concerned for Ivy as I was.

"Don't you think she would have called or done more than send that note if she were able?" I asked.

"We must think positive. Ivy wrote that she thought someone knew about her. Maybe they never revealed her identity. Maybe she is still here working and absolutely fine."

Before I could say more, Mr. Edgemere returned with two large lattes. I sniffed mine, and to be truthful, I thought it rather reckless of us to drink them. Without one moment of hesitation, Mrs. North sipped all the foam and whipped cream from the top of her cup.

"I'll just let mine cool for a second. Thank you, Mr. Edgemere." I smiled at him as I placed the mug on the desk. One of us should remain coherent in case he laced our coffee with something. However, Mrs. North appeared to be fine.

"I think we have everything we need. We'll call you when we've finished," said Mrs. North, then lowered her gaze to the papers she'd pulled from her satchel to indicate Mr. Edgemere was dismissed. When the door was firmly closed behind him, she said to me, "Go now to the top floor and find two people to send back down. Once you've escorted them here, go and see what's in all the dark corners of this place."

I said nothing in response and made my way to the top floors, noting that no one in the glass-enclosed offices, including Mr. Edgemere, seemed to be paying us the least attention. Even the workers on the floor didn't give me a second glance as I searched around, hoping Ivy would be among them. Then it dawned on me. With all her planning, Mrs. North had left out one important detail. I had not the slightest idea what Ivy looked like or if she was using a false name as Mrs. North and I were. I would only recognize her if she looked similar to her sister, Holly.

What would I do now? I couldn't exactly ask at this point. Suddenly I felt like I was in an episode of *Get Smart* instead of *Mission Impossible.* I glanced around the room. The workers, mostly women, were all average height; no one was under five feet. Of course, Ivy didn't necessarily have to be an elf. It's hard to search for someone that you have no idea what they look like.

"I'm looking for Jenn and Lisa," I said. Several women came over.

"Which Jenn and Lisa?" they all seemed to ask at once. I pretended to study a card I was carrying.

"Let's see here. Gee, her handwriting is truly horrible," I said with a chuckle. "Jenn Be..."

"That's me." A woman about my age raised her hand. "Jenny Bellman."

"Good," I said, truly pleased with myself. I knew Jennifer would be a popular name with my age group. "And then there's Lisa Le..."

"Lisa Lester? Do you mean me?" A tall, older woman stepped forward.

"Yes, you're the one," I said.

"What about Barb?" one worker called out. "She was involved in an accident here two months ago. Don't you want to speak to her?"

I blinked. "Absolutely. Her name's here. And," I had to take a chance. "Is there an Ivy?"

"Ivy?" Lisa Lester said. "She used to work in the mailroom, in the basement, but I haven't seen her around for a few days."

"Good to know," I said and led them down to meet with Mrs. North.

I am not a fan of basements and usually avoid them at all costs. Everyone with an ounce of sense knows that's where the escaped convict or murder victim will be found. I did not want to discover Ivy in the basement. I had little choice, though. Mrs. North was counting on me to help.

After leaving the women with my employer, I followed the carpeted hallway to a set of elevators. Elevators are also an item I'm not fond of. Stepping inside, I pressed the bottom button. The doors slid closed and down I went.

Barely a second later I was standing in a well-lit room that appeared to be a place where large functions might be held. There were numerous tables and chairs set up and at one end was a makeshift stage with a podium. The room was cheerfully painted in a bright green and had hanging plants that I suspected were artificial. Though there were no windows at this level, I had the sense of being outdoors. It no longer seemed a place where Freddy Kruger could be lurking.

There was a hallway opposite where I stood. I followed it down to the next large room, passing several other glass-enclosed spaces, all empty of people. The next room I entered was definitely the mailroom. Large carts were filled to the brim with letter and packages. Returns, it seemed to me.

No one was around. I went behind the counter to check out the mail cubbies that lined the wall. Most were empty. Under the counter were mailbags with envelopes spilling out. I picked one from the floor. It was addressed to Santa Claus.

"What are you doing down here?" a voice said from behind me.

I slid the envelope into my pocket. "I'm Mrs. um..." I'd forgotten who I was supposed to be.

"I don't care who you are! You shouldn't be here, especially behind my counter."

I turned around to find a young woman, maybe twenty-five or so years old, with a blonde braid laced with purple ribbon standing with her hands folded in front of her. She wore plaid tights under a yellow paisley dress. Her bright pink lips were tightly mashed together.

"Ivy?" I ventured.

"Get away from the counter," she said, taking a step toward me.

"I'm here from the um, Safety and Health Workers. And, oh yeah, I'm Kelly, I mean Kristina Kelly. We... my boss and I... are evaluating the working conditions of this establishment and we'd like to speak to you."

"To me? You want to speak to me? Does Mr. Edgemere know you're down here?" she asked.

"You're Ivy, right?" I was unsure if I should reveal the true nature of our business. Suppose she wasn't Ivy, or the Ivy we were searching for? "Yes, he's well aware of our project today."

"I'm Ivy, but I'm not to leave my station, so anything you want to ask me, you'll have to do it here." She pushed one of the mail bags further under the counter with her foot.

I was unsure how to proceed. It was possible there could be more than one young woman named Ivy. It had become a popular name in recent years, along with Fern and Lily. With the outfit she was wearing, I could totally see her working for Mrs. North. "Maybe you could start with describing your daily duties," I said.

"There's not much to it, and it's all kind of boring," she said, still keeping an eye on the mail bags.

"How long have you worked here?" I asked.

"Not very long, maybe a month or two."

"Where were you previously employed?" I pretended to record her answers on the card I was carrying.

"Why do you need to know that?" She lowered her voice and looked carefully around the room.

"No reason. You just said this job was boring and I wondered what type of place you may have worked in before. That's all. Maybe it would be better if my boss came down and spoke to you. Her name is Hedda Nelson."

Ivy narrowed her eyes. "You work for Hedda Nelson?" The young woman looked around all sides of her, then eased closer to me. "What's the word?" she whispered.

"The word?"

"Yes, the word."

I shook my head.

"The secret password, you know," she muttered through gritted teeth.

"I'm sorry, I don't know. She didn't give me a word." Then I too scanned the room. "Is it Santa? Presents?" I had no idea.

"Good grief, that's close enough, I suppose." Ivy grabbed hold of my elbow and yanked me toward the hallway. "First off, tell Hedda to stop using the same name for all her missions. Secondly, tell her I have the letters and I'm trying to mail them out a few at a time. If too many are missing, they'll get suspicious. I still can't get hold of the list yet. I'm sure it's in the owner's office."

"You think Edgemere has them?" I asked.

"He's just a front. Somebody else owns this place, but I don't know who. Look, I can't say much more. They already think something's up with me and are watching," but before she could finish, we heard footsteps coming our way. "Hide," she said and pushed me toward the carts.

Where? The other offices had glass walls. I spotted a large canvas basket bulk truck only half filled. It looked like the type of cart they used to haul laundry within hotels. I wasted no time and dove in, covering myself the best I could with letters and packages.

"Talking to yourself again?" I heard Mr. Edgemere say.

Ivy's reply was muffled and lost to me.

"Why haven't these packages gone out yet?" he asked, and I felt the basket move ever so slightly.

"I was getting ready to put it out now," Ivy said more clearly. The cart jerked and a few packages tumbled on my head.

"Those women haven't been down here, have they?"

"No one's been here 'cept you." Ivy's voice was close, and I knew she now had hold of the cart that began to move, first gently then with some speed. "Stay down, stay down, Sweet Chariot," she sang as we moved along.

"Those are not the words," I heard Mr. Edgemere call out. "It's *swing low*. Stupid girl."

The cart hit a bump and I suspected we were now in the elevator. "Alright, you can come out now," Ivy said and helped to pull me up. "Stand here in the shadow then wait to get off on the next floor. I don't want the others to see us together. Where's Mrs. North?"

"First floor near the entrance," I said, smoothing the wrinkles from my dress.

"Good. I'll pass by so she sees I'm okay, but you tell her I'm no closer to locating the list. She may have a better chance now that she's here." The elevator doors opened, and Ivy pushed the canvas basket off. I stood tightly against the wall until she was out.

I decided to ride up to the third floor and gather a few more employees. Mr. Edgemere was in the office with Mrs. North when I returned.

"Haven't you enough information?" he was saying to her as I entered. "The two of you have disrupted our entire workday, and for what?"

Mrs. North looked pointedly at me. I nodded slightly. "Very well," she said to him in that brisk, clipped tone of hers. "Our job is not to interfere with your work, only to see that your employees are being treated properly. Your staff has given you a glowing review. I don't see that we need to trouble you any further." Mrs. North promptly shoved her papers in her satchel, hoisted the strap onto her shoulder, and strolled past Mr. Edgemere.

The man seemed stunned and stood open-mouthed as we left the room. It was probably the mention of a glowing review. He had to know that was untrue.

Mrs. North waited until we had pulled away from the parking lot to tell me what she'd learned. "Those poor women are worked to death," she said snatching a bag of candy cane cigarettes from her purse and pressing in the car's lighter. "I truly don't know how they manage. Most of them have families with young children. They work all day then go to pick up children from school or sitters, prepare meals, and oversee homework all the while sorting laundry and cleaning house. I'm exhausted just hearing about it."

I thought of my own mother and how distracted she always seemed. Never any time for me or the things I wanted to do. My marriages had not produced any children and for this I was always thankful because I never wanted to take a chance I'd repeat my mother's mistakes. I'd never considered the other roles she'd had to take part in.

"Natalie, are you listening to me?" Mrs. North stepped hard on the brake, and we jolted forward in our seats.

"Yes, yes, of course. I was just thinking about the women we saw. Did you notice Edgemere's expression when you mentioned the glowing remarks?"

"Yes, I knew we better skedaddle after that," Mrs. North laughed, and a cloud of peppermint smoke escaped her mouth and nose. "He's wretched and I'll be reporting him to the Better Business Bureau and any other agency I can think of. He's definitely receiving coal in his stocking this year. I'll make a specific note to Nico about it."

"Did you see Ivy?" I asked. "She told me there is someone above Edgemere, the owner of the company, who has the list. She seems to think you will have a better chance of finding the list than she does."

"I don't think we are going to be able to gain access under the same guise again. This time we'll have to go the Saint Nick way."

"The Saint Nick way? What's that?"

"Under the cover of night, from the rooftop, of course," she said with a smile. "You'll love it."

"I'm afraid I won't."

Chapter 4

When we arrived back at the house, Nico was busy waxing his surfboard. The temperature had dropped considerably, and a gray sky filled with dark clouds hung menacingly above us. I couldn't even imagine how frigid the ocean must be, but no matter the weather, Nico pulled on his wetsuit and took to the waves. I shuddered at the thought.

"Nice shopping trip?" he asked as we piled out of the car. Much to my surprise, the trunk was filled with shopping bags from the local dress shops.

"Yes, darling. It was fabulous," answered Mrs. North, planting a kiss on his cheek. "Our dear Natalie was in desperate need of a wardrobe update, weren't you?" she nodded toward me.

"Oh, absolutely," I agreed and helped her to haul the bags into the house.

"Take these to your room," she said. "Anything that doesn't fit, leave in the hall and I'll have them returned."

"All of this is for me?" I asked, too stunned to move any further. "I can't afford, I mean, I..."

"It's a gift, darling. It's what I do, you know," she said and waved me away with her hand.

I lugged the bags upstairs and pulled them onto the bed. Each one was stuffed with sweaters, tights, skirts, and slacks. Much of it looked similar to the outfit Ivy had worn. I wasn't sure I could pull off striped tights and floral dresses at my age. I couldn't remember the last time I'd bought anything new, let alone an entire wardrobe of clothes. I tried each piece on and was happy with the way they suited me.

I swirled in front of the mirror until Mrs. North called out, "Natalie, will you be spending the rest of the evening admiring yourself? You know, we do have much more to accomplish."

I begrudgingly left my new clothes across the bed and went off to Mrs. North's office. "Thank you so much for the clothes," I said. "They're really lovely and nothing I would have ever bought for myself."

"I remember when you were a little girl how you loved all things Laura Ashley. Then at some point you took on that horrid grunge look. So disappointing. It will be nice to see you in some color for a change."

I smiled at her. How funny to hear about color as she sat once again in her silver, gray, and white. She looked at ease in whatever clothing she wore, comfortable in her own skin. Maybe that was the secret I was missing. I'd yet to be comfortable with myself.

"What's on the agenda this evening?" I asked and settled in at the small desk near her.

"First, I'll need to answer these letters from the paper. After dinner we'll discuss Plan Sleigh Ride."

Here might have been a good time to tell her I was not a fan of heights, nor had I ever been on a plane. I could only assume that this sleigh would be flying and landing on top of The Everywhere Corporation building.

"I know what you're thinking," Mrs. North said, and I had no doubt. "But you won't even realize we're off the ground, and we'll arrive at our mission in seconds. You'll be astonished at the speed this thing can travel."

"What about the reindeer?" I asked.

"Darling, they are just for show. We won't need them on this trip." She put on her glasses and checked her calendar. "I was thinking not tomorrow night, but the next would be best to tackle this. What do you think?"

I stared at her. "Me? What would I know about breaking into a complex?"

"We are not *breaking in,* as you so vulgarly put it. We will be paying them an unexpected visit, that's all. We'll slip in, retrieve what is rightfully ours, and leave. No one will know. Well, at least until they go looking for the list. We must also get word to Ivy so she isn't accused of taking it."

"How will we tell her?" I wanted to know.

"We will send a Dear Santa letter, of course."

That did not sound like the most solid idea to me. Suppose the letter got lost? The mail had not been the most reliable in the last few years. Or what if it arrived, but fell into someone else's hands other than Ivy's?

"Shouldn't we call her?" I asked. "I think she's living downstairs in that mailroom. She told me they were watching her. Do you think this company is doing something more serious than stealing lists from Santa? I mean, really, she seemed pretty afraid."

"Natalie, you still have not grasped the seriousness of this situation. I know to you it all seems rather silly, all this searching for a simple list. These people are evil. Their concern is about what goes in their pockets. People don't matter to them. It's profit and what they will get. They will stop at nothing to take what they want, and apparently, they want everything.

"We're going to give it a few days, just in case Edgemere is suspicious of us, which I think he was. Then on Friday night, when the company is closed for the weekend, we will go."

I tossed and turned that night, unable to get Ivy from my mind. Part of our plan had to be to get her out of there, along with the list.

Mrs. North was serious about her night mission. She sent me a black leotard to try on. I put a robe over it and walked down to her office after she insisted on seeing how it fit.

"I feel like an out of shape ballerina," I said as I came in.

She was wearing something similar. "I think we rather look like Eartha Kitt and Julie Newmar."

"We don't have ears," I said with a laugh. "If we wear boots, we could be Mrs. Peel." I rather liked the thought of imitating Diana Rigg from one of my favorite childhood shows.

"Now, I like that idea. It's so nice to be able to chat with someone who enjoys television as much as I do. Nico has only watched *The Endless Summer* and *Point Break*. Though I must confess that Keanu Reeves is very yummy." Mrs. North nearly purred as she said this.

I had to admit this was fun, and not conversation I was able to have with many people. Lady M despised television, even though her true fame had come from daytime serials. My husband, during either of our marriages, hadn't been interested in the programs I watched. Actually, thinking back, he didn't have much interest in anything I did. Even Mrs. Doolittle, whom I dearly loved, wasn't a fan of television. She spent her evenings listening to WDDE on the radio, her favorite show being *This American Life*.

"Here are your gloves and a knit cap. It'll be chilly." Mrs. North balled the gloves into the hat and tossed them to me. Before I could catch them, her office door flung open.

"Look at the two of you," laughed Nico, and I noticed his belly didn't shake like a bowl full of jelly. "What are you all dressed up for?"

"You're going to ruin our surprise, darling," Mrs. North said and put her arms around his neck. "We're planning our costumes for Halloween, of course."

"I should have known," said Nico, planting a kiss on her cheek. "I was wondering if you ladies would care to join me for a cocktail before dinner."

"Don't let him fool you, Natalie. He's going to make us one of his horrid concoctions that will involve wheat grass and some strange fruit no one's ever heard of." Mrs. North kissed him back. "But we will humor him."

"No, honest, I have limes and rum," he said, then winked at me.

"I like limes and rum," I said. "Let me change and I'll be right back." I hurried out and up to my room. They were looking rather cozy, so I thought I should take my time getting back.

After thirty minutes I returned and found them in the living room drinking some sort of frozen daiquiri. I accepted a chilled glass from Nico.

"We were beginning to think you'd ditched us," said Mrs. North. "I was going to send Holly to find you."

"Where is Holly? Won't she be joining us?" I peered into the other room, but the rest of the house was dark.

"Holly's been rather quiet since Ivy ran away," Nico said.

Mrs. North and I exchanged a glance.

"Ivy?" I asked.

"Surely Bee has told you about our Ivy. She ran off several weeks ago. We were shocked and upset. Holly and Ivy are sisters. Those girls are like daughters to us." Nico's voice was rough. He looked away from me and at the fire that was blazing in the grate. After a few seconds, he continued. "She left a short note but didn't actually say why she wanted to leave. I can't imagine what would make her go."

"Darling, she's a grown woman. I think she'll return as soon as she's seen a bit of the world." Mrs.

North went to Nico and rubbed his shoulder. “Let’s have some dinner, you’ll feel better. It’s never good to drink on an empty stomach. Afterwards, Natalie and I will watch *Point Break* with you.”

This made Nico smile. “Trying to get Natalie to join your Keanu Reeves fan club, are you?”

“You know me too well, darling!” Mrs. North brushed her fingers over Nico’s collar as she passed him. “Let me make us a bite to eat,” she said, before going off to the kitchen.

Nico turned to me once Mrs. North was out of earshot. “Thank you, Natalie,” he said.

“For what?” I could feel my cheeks coloring and hoped he couldn’t read me as easily as his wife. Too late I remembered her saying he was actually the more intuitive.

“Oh, for everything, for just being here. I think you are the right person for Bee. She’s been down in the dumps, not only since Ivy left. It started before then. I know I’m to blame for some of it. Bee wasn’t exactly thrilled with the idea of moving here. She wanted to stick it out at the, well, at our previous home.”

I wanted to tell him that I knew who he was, but then I suppose I’d have to admit why Mrs. North revealed so much to me. “I enjoy my job,” I said instead. “I’ve been a personal assistant for many years, and I really like Mrs. North.”

“Well, I for one am glad you’re happy here. Anyone who keeps Bee happy is good with me,” Nico said. “Enjoy the rest of your drink. I think I’ll see if I can assist my wife. We’ll call you when supper is ready." He smiled at me, and I noticed for the first time he had a dimple in his right cheek.

I sat back in my chair and sipped the last of my cocktail. I'd certainly learned my lesson with Lady M and Felix, but boy, in another life, Nico would certainly be the kind of man I'd want.

Dinner was a simple salad with smoked salmon. After the dishes had been cleared, Mrs. North made good on her promise, and we watched *Point Break*. I had to agree with her about Keanu Reeves. I'd be watching this film again.

"Tomorrow we'll cement our plans," Mrs. North whispered to me as I made my way upstairs.

I wasn't too keen on the idea of breaking into The Everywhere Corporation. There was something creepy about the place. It had a Stepford Wives vibe about it. I was especially worried about wearing the leotard. I did not ever want to be seen in that thing. Mrs. North might be tall and trim and looking fabulous in everything she wore, but I did not have the same genetics. I looked like what I was, a middle-aged woman. Mrs. North, on the other hand, was a goddess.

"Get up," a voice said. At first, I thought I was dreaming. My room was dark, and I couldn't make out who was speaking, but felt the someone sit on the side of the bed. "Come on, she's waiting for you."

I switched on my lamp to find Holly at my side. "Who? What time is it?"

"No matter. Get dressed. Mrs. North needs you. She's in quite a panic." Holly's long golden plaits swung behind her as she left the room.

"Good grief, what now?" I still hadn't remembered to put the mouthwash at my bedside, so I swished a bit of water in my mouth, grabbed a shirt dress from my closet, and dashed downstairs.

Mrs. North was sitting behind her desk with the same panic-stricken expression she had worn the other night. "Natalie, I am in a bind." She waved me to come closer.

"What's wrong? What happened?" I asked, going to her side.

"It's Nico," she whispered, pointing to the office next door. "He's over there right now searching for the list. I've hid his glasses so he's really struggling. Natalie, I feel terrible. In nearly two hundred years of marriage, I've never lied to my husband. Now within a few weeks, I have so many stories going even I am finding it hard to remember what's true."

"Why not just tell him what's happened? You can skip over the part about you being in possession of the list and just say it was stolen," I said.

"I don't think I can. It's too late for that. We need to move our mission up," said Mrs. North.

"Okay," I said, but still thought this wasn't the best idea. "When?"

"Now, right this moment. Get your tights and leotard on."

"Now? How can we leave? Won't he miss you and wonder where you're going?" I was not ready for this.

"He's so absorbed. He won't miss me. I'll meet you out back near the garage. Be there in ten minutes."

I hurried past Nico's office door where I could hear desk drawers being slammed shut. Once back in my room, I slipped out of my dress and struggled into my mission outfit. I really hoped I'd never have to wear this thing again. Grabbing my knit cap and gloves that Mrs. North had provided, I took a black hoodie from my drawer and brought that along as well. The nights were getting rather chilly, and if my legs couldn't be warm at least my arms would be.

Mrs. North was standing in front of the garage door with a flashlight in one hand and a candy cane cigarette in the other. "Ready?" she asked.

"No, I'm still not sure this is the right way to do this. And we haven't contacted Ivy."

"We will worry about that when we get there. Come on." She crushed her cigarette under the heel of her thigh-high boot.

I looked down at my own feet and the paint splattered sneakers on them. Mrs. North looked elegant in everything she wore. I followed her into the garage feeling like a slob.

She switched on the flashlight, or torch as she called it, and we made our way to a large object covered with a blue drop cloth. We each grabbed an end and pulled. The cloth fell to the ground to reveal what appeared to me to be a snow mobile. It was bright, sparkly red.

Mrs. North hopped in and I slid in next to her. The seats were warm and covered in white wool like the insides of my slippers. “Where are the reindeer?” I asked.

“Reindeer?” Mrs. North wrinkled her nose.

“Yeah, you know Dasher, Dancer, Prancer and the others?”

“Really, Natalie, you are much too involved with make-believe. Have you ever been in the woods and seen all the deer droppings? Imagine them flying across the sky. There would be more than snow falling on Christmas Eve.” Mrs. North turned on the vehicle.

“Must you ruin all my childhood illusions?” I asked her as we puttered out of the garage and into the night.

“They are *delusions*, darling,” she said, just as we were jolted into the sky.

I held tight to the leather strap fastened over my lap as we climbed higher into the sky. My pulse raced and my ears popped. The moon was hiding behind clouds that occasionally shifted to reveal an eerie light. There was no sound from the world below us, or it could have just been my ears were so clogged I could no longer hear.

Before I’d fully adjusted, we were landing on the roof of The Everywhere Corporation. “That was fast,” I said.

“Of course, it was. How else would we make it around the world in one night?” Mrs. North said as she stepped out of the vehicle.

I followed on shaky legs. Heights and flying were definitely not my thing. The parking lot below us was empty, and only the exterior lights shone from the building. I looked around but couldn't see any way of getting inside from the roof.

"Okay, I give. How are we getting in there from here?"

Much to my horror, Mrs. North pulled a coiled rope from behind the seat. She tied one end to a metal hook near the edge of the roof and gave it two or three hard yanks.

"I'll go down first and open the window," she said, tying a length of the rope around her waist.

"You've got to be kidding me," I said, afraid to even look over the side of the building.

"You'll be perfectly safe, darling. Trust me. The window isn't any more than two feet below us."

"I can't, I just can't." My knees began to knock together, and my stomach turned over. I was afraid I'd have to use the bathroom. "You act like we're some sort of cat burglars or something."

"Natalie, how did you think we were going to get inside?" she asked, her hands on her hips. "Please don't tell me you thought we'd slide down a chimney. Who do you think we are, Mary Poppins and Bert?"

"No," I said, but actually had thought Mrs. North would have some magical way of entering the building. I hated to admit I was disappointed. First, no flying reindeer and now this. "I'm not a good climber, and I'm not good with heights." I stared down at my shoes. Had I realized, I too would have worn boots, but on second thought, the only boots I had were snow boots.

Mrs. North glanced at the rope, then back at me. “Natalie, you will be fine, I promise. Look at me,” she said. “No, really look at me.”

I did. I searched her eyes, and a calm came over me. My heart began to beat at its normal pace and my knees became still. As if in a trance, I watched as she lowered herself off the roof and down the wall. A few seconds later, she called my name and I grabbed hold of the rope and went to meet her. I don’t remember climbing down the wall or into the window. We were standing in a darkened office when I became fully aware of my surroundings.

“How did you do that?” I asked.

Mrs. North shook her head. “I didn’t do a thing,” she answered. “Now let’s find the list and get out of here.”

“What about Ivy?” I whispered.

“You search for the list while I get her,” Mrs. North said.

“No, I know exactly where to find her.” Before Mrs. North could disagree, I turned the lock on the door and slipped out into the hall. It was much darker out there. I slid my phone from my hoodie’s pocket and switched on the flashlight app. It had been on a few seconds when I heard footsteps coming toward me.

Where to hide? I flipped off my phone light and stood very still like a child who thinks stillness means no one can see them.

I saw a flicker of light, heard a jingle of keys, and realized it must be a night watchman. Careful not to make a sound, I shifted closer to the wall. The footsteps grew closer. I had no way of knowing where I could hide. Then the clouds shifted, and moonlight filled the room. There was a large desk in the corner behind some worktables. I wasted no time climbing under the desk.

The person was now in the room with me, their flashlight beam shifting back and forth across the floor. I caught sight of striped tights. It wasn't a night watchman, it was Ivy. I let out a small sigh and began to slide out from under the desk when I heard someone else approach.

"Did you find her?" a male voice asked.

"No. You told me she was staying here. Are you lying to me?"

I peered out from where I hid. The girl in the striped tights was now illuminated by the moonlight. It was Holly, not Ivy, who spoke. The man stood with his back to me, and once again I couldn't see his face.

"Mrs. North is very upset. I think she knows the list is missing. She and the new assistant have been locked in her office all night. I must find Ivy before Mrs. North learns what she's done." Holly started walking toward the office where Mrs. North was searching.

Had Ivy been the one to take the list then pretend to go and retrieve it? She had seemed truly frightened when I spoke to her, but who was she really afraid of? Someone here? Or Mrs. North?

"I told you, we will find your sister. I wish I'd never let you talk me into breaking in here, though," the man said. Their voices became fainter as they moved down the hallway. Surely Mrs. North must have heard them coming by now.

"Ivy, where are you and what have you done?" I said under my breath.

The clouds covered the moon and once again I was in complete darkness. Easing myself out from under the desk, I crept along the hall, feeling my way as I went. I could no longer hear Holly or see any reflection from their flashlights. Unfortunately, Mrs. North was not where I left her.

"Mrs. North," I whispered into the darkness before feeling safe enough to turn my light back on. She was nowhere. "Great. This is just great." There was no rope and the window we had come through was closed tightly. I must have taken too long, and she decided to look for me and Ivy.

The office door opened without a creak. I peered down the hallway, but still saw and heard nothing. I crept out, keeping my light down low. The building was still. Mrs. North was good at disappearing. I suspected that some of my dreams of her weren't dreams at all; she'd actually been in my room.

I came to a staircase and stopped to listen before proceeding down. It seemed I was on the second floor where the women packed the merchandise. Cautiously, I held my phone up and let the light hit all the dark corners of the room. No one was here. Where could Mrs. North be? For that matter, where was Ivy and why hadn't Holly been able to find her?

A light tapping on the window startled me. I turned to find Mrs. North dangling from a rope. It didn't look as if the rope was secure as she swung back and forth. Wasting no time, I ran to the windows, but there was no way to open them. "Hang on!" I said, my face pressed up to the glass.

She smiled and waved, not seeming stressed at all. "Meet you out front, darling," she called. Then she was gone.

It seemed I'd have to make it downstairs without being seen. My rubber-soled shoes squeaked as I tiptoed to the front door. I wondered if I should go to the mailroom to see if Ivy might be hiding there, but thought better of it. Mrs. North seemed relaxed and happy. I could only surmise that meant she'd found the list. That was the mission, after all.

As I reached the door, it occurred to me there could be an alarm. I debated on what to do, but before I could decide someone came up behind me.

"Hey! You!" a man's voice called out.

Alarm or not, I pushed through the front doors and took off running. As I turned onto the long driveway, I heard a slight buzzing sound nearing.

"Natalie," shouted Mrs. North. "Hop in." She slowed down but did not stop. Reaching out a hand, she grabbed hold of my wrist and yanked me into the vehicle. Up into the sky we went as I adjusted myself in the seat.

When I looked down, a small man stood staring up at us.

Chapter 5

The ride home was silent. Mrs. North smoked one candy cane after another. The house was dark when we snuck in. We went to Mrs. North's office, and she poured us each a shot of Peppermint Schnapps. It burned going down, but I needed it.

"The list wasn't there, at least I couldn't find it," she said, picking up the bottle for a second shot.

"But you looked so happy when I saw you outside the window," I said.

"I may not have found the list, but I did discover who is in charge at The Everywhere Corporation."

"Who?" I asked.

"Let me pour you another drink," said Mrs. North. "You may need it."

I let her give me a little more. "Are you going to tell me?"

"Do the initials V.D. mean anything to you?"

I nearly spit out my drink. "Yes, but it's nothing I've ever experienced myself. Though there was this time when Lady M was seeing this actor and Felix and I..."

"For goodness's sake, Natalie, I'm not talking about venereal disease. Who do you know whose first name begins with the letter V and their last name starts with a D?" Mrs. North shook her head as she sat down. "I can't believe you would even think I met a sexually transmitted disease. Really, Natalie!"

"V..." I put my glass on the table. "Violet Doolittle. Do you mean to tell me you believe Mrs. Doolittle is the owner of The Everywhere Corporation? How can that be?"

"You shouldn't be so shocked. Violet is a very capable businesswoman. She's been running that temp agency nearly as long as you've been alive. She learned from the best, if I do say so myself." Mrs. North sat back in her desk chair and crossed her arms. "Given her background, though, I don't understand why she would want to take the list and hurt Nico in this way."

"But you told me after people leave the North Pole their memories of that time fade. Maybe she doesn't remember growing up there, or her family's long history of working for Santa."

"That's true, but now knowing Violet owns this company puts the theft in a new light."

"She was determined that I accept this job, and did want to hear about everything, especially about you. I think a visit to Mrs. Doolittle is in order. I'm going first thing in the morning," I said. I headed toward the door. "I'm going to need some sleep first."

"Natalie, be careful with her. I'll keep my eye on you the best I can, but I believe there's more to Violet Doolittle than we know."

Halloween morning was crisp, colder than the days before. As I walked through town, I noticed the shops had changed out their window displays from leaves and pumpkins to all things Christmas. I shook my head. Before trick or treaters had even received their candy, the stores were on to the next holiday. Businesses were anxious to coax the consumers to spend big bucks. Everything Mrs. North had said was more obvious than ever to me.

The warmth I usually felt walking up the boarding house steps was replaced by a burning in the pit of my stomach. I shouldn't have been so surprised. Every woman I'd idolized—my mother, Lady M, and now Mrs. Doolittle—all turned out to be a villain in my story.

I could smell bread baking as I entered the front door. A woman I'd never seen before rushed past me without a word. What's-her-name was drinking a cup of coffee at the table and reading the *Beach Banner*. She folded it up when she noticed me.

"Oh, hello there," she said, a smile forming on her thin lips. "We were just talking about you and wondering how you were doing with the advice columnist."

I poured myself a cup of coffee and sat across from her. "You were? You and who else?"

"Me, of course," said Mrs. Doolittle entering the breakfast nook with a plate of hot bread and a basket full of jams and honey. "How are you, dearie? I thought I'd be seeing you before now. The great Mrs. North keeps you busy then, does she?"

"Yes, we've been swamped with mail, among other things," I said, eyeing up the bread. I did miss Mrs. Doolittle's cooking.

"As anxious as I am to get the scoop, I've got to run. I don't want to be late for my first day at Browse About. See you later." What's-her-name took one last sip of coffee before rushing out the door.

"She's a pleasant girl, but not as punctual as she should be. This is her final chance. The other stores don't want to put up with her tardiness or her absent-mindedness. I can't say I blame them. Not all my workers are as reliable as you, dearie." Mrs. Doolittle refilled my cup and slid the bread plate toward me.

How could I refuse? I took one slice and slathered on a spoonful of raspberry jam. "If all else fails, I've heard The Everywhere Corporation is hiring for the holidays. Maybe she could find work there." I watched for Mrs. Doolittle's reaction, but she just ate her bread without looking at me. So I continued. "A few workers from The Everywhere Corp have been writing Mrs. North asking for her advice."

"Advice on what?" Mrs. Doolittle asked between bites.

"They say their boss asks too much of them, and that there have been accidents. They said that the owner of the company is heartless and overworks them." I stopped at that, thinking I was laying it on too thick.

"You know, that's how those companies are, dearie, never much thought to the little people who work for them." She looked over at me, her green eyes twinkling, but there was no hint of a smile in them.

There was no sign of her dimples or her good humor. "What advice does Mrs. North give these sad, underappreciated workers? I haven't seen it in the paper."

"She's still answering them, as far as I know. Mrs. North doesn't talk to me about them. My job is to sort the letters, then someone at the paper types the answers up for her." That sounded like the safest thing to say.

"If this is such a bad place to work, why would you recommend me sending workers there?" asked Mrs. Doolittle.

"I just thought since it was a temporary position, it might be okay." My reasoning sounded weak, even to me. I changed topics. "How have things been here? Did the waitress at Robin Hood's have her baby?"

Mrs. Doolittle said nothing for a few minutes, only sipped her coffee and watched me from over the rim of her cup. "No baby as of yet," she finally said. "Everyone but what's-her-name, as you call her, has found permanent jobs. She's the only team member I have left."

Hearing this made my heart hurt. "I'm sure with the start of the new year you'll find more people to work at the agency."

"Mm, yes, I suppose. What's it like inside the North house? How's Mr. North?" Mrs. Doolittle placed her cup in its saucer and stared at me. I wondered if she had the ability to read me like Mrs. North did.

"It's lonely," I said honestly.

Mrs. Doolittle smiled, revealing her dimples. "Tell me all about it, dearie."

"Mrs. North is all business. I eat alone, every meal, on a tray that's left for me in the kitchen. They're into health food, so there's no waffles or fresh baked bread. My room is beautiful, but I don't have much down time to enjoy it."

"How did you happen to get away this morning?" she asked.

"I'm supposed to be running errands for Mrs. North. She and her husband are away for the day."

"You like it there. I can see it in your face. I wonder, Natalie, if you've really been searching for a job or if you are trying to find a home."

These words brought tears to my eyes. "I'll always think of this place as home," I told her and stood to leave. As I walked down the hallway, I glanced at the photos on the wall. I'd seen them at least a hundred times. The one I'd always liked best had a new meaning. In it she stood with a little man, the same man I'd seen last night as I was getting away. I'd always thought this had been some snowy holiday, but I now knew it was the North Pole. Mrs. Doolittle had not forgotten a thing.

"How long are we going to wait?" I whispered to Mrs. North as we both sat squished under her desk.

"As long as it takes. She'll be here, I'm sure of it."

I wasn't as sure as Mrs. North. Why she would think Mrs. Doolittle would decide now to break into

North Pole Beach was beside me. "Were you listening in on my conversation with Mrs. Doolittle?"

"Santa's not the only one who knows if you've been bad or good," said Mrs. North and she chuckled softly. "I'm not giving away any company secrets, not even to you. At least not yet."

"There must be more to your former relationship with Mrs. Doolittle than you're telling me," I said.

"It's not my relationship with..." Before Mrs. North could finish her sentence, we heard a small tapping in the hall.

I put my finger to my lips and Mrs. North nodded. I knew that tapping sound. It came from the kitten-heeled boots Mrs. Doolittle liked to wear.

The office door creaked open. "Hello?" her tiny voice called out.

I held my breath, afraid to move an inch.

Mrs. Doolittle closed the office door and began sifting through the letters I had piled earlier on Mrs. North's worktable. She took a stack of them and sat in a chair to read.

Mrs. North stood and pulled the chain of the desk lamp flooding the room with light. "Good afternoon, Violet. I do hope you have found what you're looking for. Maybe I could help, if you don't see what you need there."

I peered out from under the desk, still too afraid to move. Mrs. Doolittle seemed genuinely shocked. Her mouth hung part way open, and her eyes were wide. The papers she held trembled in her hands.

"I, well I..." she started to say.

Mrs. North walked around to the front of the desk, leaned against it blocking my view, and lit a candy cane. "How rude of me. Would you care for one?" she asked Mrs. Doolittle, and I could hear the candy canes being shook out of the box.

I slid slightly over and peeked around Mrs. North's legs. Mrs. Doolittle accepted a light, then took a long drag off her cigarette. In my mind, I could hear Mrs. North's voice. *"Stay where you are,"* she told me.

"Let's not play anymore games, Violet. What is it that you want?" Mrs. North asked.

Mrs. Doolittle stared down at the growing ash at the tip of her cigarette before answering. "I can never have what I want, so I'll take what you want instead."

Mrs. North stood straighter, the creases in her pant legs unfolding. "You have no idea what I want," she said in a measured voice.

"I thought I'd never see you again," Mrs. Doolittle said. "Then one morning there was a man surfing, an older man. I knew right away it was your Nico."

I didn't like the way Mrs. Doolittle had emphasized the word *your*.

"He's in pretty good shape for an elderly man. My Herbie is at least ten years younger, and he's as broken down as a man can be. After that first day, I began to see him every morning and that made me wonder why he was here. Why of all the places in the world he could go, did he choose Rehoboth Beach?"

"It's not that hard to figure out," Mrs. North said. "He's in semi-retirement. He wanted to learn to surf, and you know we'd never survive in a warmer climate."

Mrs. Doolittle seemed to think this over. "All these years it's taken me to get over what you did to me. I finally found a place I could be myself, a place I didn't get overlooked or ignored. A place where I didn't have to compete with my sister."

I banged my head on the desk when I heard that. Mrs. North and Mrs. Doolittle were sisters?

"What was that?" Mrs. Doolittle asked.

"I think Natalie has given herself another concussion. Come out, darling. You may as well join us."

I really didn't want to, but I was good at following orders. "Hello," I said to Mrs. Doolittle as I crawled out from under the desk.

The disappointment on her face caused me to look away. I wasn't sure why I was ashamed, but I still felt that way.

"You know, I'd nearly forgotten my life at the castle. Seeing Nico brought it all back. Herbie started The Everywhere Corporation not long before I realized Nico was in town. It took me a while to figure out you were Mrs. North. That was silly of me. You think I'd recognize my own maiden name and with Nico in town, put it all together. As usual, I was slow."

"I thought you forgot about us like the others had done," said Mrs. North.

"I tried, especially after I'd met Herbie. Seeing Nico brought back the memory of how he used me, pretended to like me, just to get closer to you. That's why I left. I couldn't stand to see you together. I came by one afternoon and Ivy let me in. I could see right away she remembered me. She sat me here in your office while she went to make tea. For a few minutes, I thought I might even forgive you, but then I saw the list. After all these years, my name was still on the Naughty list." Mrs. Doolittle balled her tiny fist and punched the arms of the chair. "That made me so mad. I took it and left"

"Well now, darling, you had been naughty, hadn't you? It took us over a week to find the reindeer you let out of the barn. Then there was the Ex-Lax in Nico's chocolate chip cookies. You can't expect Santa to ever forget having to wear adult diapers on his Christmas Eve journey. What a night that was!"

"I was angry, upset. You married the man I loved, always loved. Hearing Ivy say my name was still on that list after all these years was the final blow. Herbie's company had been successful. I knew then I could take Christmas from Nico and through that take what you valued most... Nico's happiness."

"Violet, you were a little girl. I had no idea you were in love with Nico. I thought you loved him the way all children did. That's why we couldn't understand why you behaved so badly after we got married." Mrs. North stood and went over to her sister. "Then Ivy knew all along who had the list?"

"I have the list," Nico said, entering the room. "Violet, it's behavior like this that keeps your name in the Naughty column."

"It's not her fault," said Mrs. North. "I took the list from your office. I wanted to write to the children and ask them to send you more letters."

"There are hundreds of letters in the mailroom at The Everywhere Corporation," I said. "I've seen them."

Mrs. Doolittle stood and tried to squeeze past Nico. "It doesn't matter anymore. Kids today and their parents will order from us. You're the past, we are the future."

"Violet, please stay," Mrs. North said, her voice softening.

Nico watched the two women, not saying a word, but also not moving to let Mrs. Doolittle pass.

"Now you want me to stay?" Mrs. Doolittle laughed. "It was you who sent me away."

"I didn't mean it to be forever. I only wanted you to have what your friends had, an education in the best schools, to see the world." Mrs. North reached out her hand, but then drew it quickly back.

"You wanted me to have what everyone else had, but not what you had. You've always wanted all the love for yourself, first Mama's and Papa's, then Nico's. Now you even have Natalie's. You told me on the phone it was a temporary position, but I knew you would keep her." Mrs. Doolittle finally turned her eyes to me. "I truly wanted what was best for you, dearie, honest I did."

I believed her, but only so far. "I know," I said. "But you also wanted me to tell you what was happening here."

Mrs. Doolittle bowed her head and stared at her feet.

"Instead of scheming, Violet, you should have come and talked to us. Years ago, you could have said at any time you were interested in leaving the community." Nico's voice was harsh, but then he looked over at his wife, and sighed. "Violet," he gently lifted her chin with his finger. "I've known all along where you were and what you were doing. I'm Santa. Did you really think anything escaped my attention?" He laughed deeply, in exactly the way Santa should.

For the first time, I saw him as the figure children around the world adored. His eyes twinkled, and his face glowed. Everything about him radiated love and understanding.

"Bee and I weren't sure what you remembered," he said to her. "When Ivy left, I thought her memories were beginning to fade as well. Now she may be lost to us."

Mrs. Doolittle pulled away from Nico. "I will return your precious list, but I can't change any of the other things I've done. The world will move on and the two of you will be stuck in a time forgotten."

Mrs. North didn't look as relieved as I thought she would. She seemed even more troubled.

"The list will be returned," I said and touched her arm to reassure her.

"All this secrecy was about the list?" Nico asked his wife. "I make copies of everything."

"Then what were you looking for the other night?" Mrs. North asked.

"My cell phone, like always." He laughed again.

Everything seemed to be turning out alright, but then Holly burst through the door.

"I thought he was my friend, helping me to find Ivy, but he took her!" She grabbed hold of Nico's sleeve. "He's working for that man at the big company. We must save her."

"What man at the company? My Herbie?" asked Mrs. Doolittle.

"No, the balding man," Holly said and raced from the room.

We all followed her, even Mrs. Doolittle.

"I told Herbie not to hire him. That man never listens to me."

"Take the car," said Mrs. North and threw me the keys. "Nico and I will meet you there."

Mrs. Doolittle slid into the passenger seat as I started the car. Holly was ahead of us, roaring out onto the street on a Vespa. The Norths started up the snowmobile and I glimpsed them gliding into the air in my rearview mirror. They would most certainly arrive first to The Everywhere Corporation.

"I never intended for things to be this way," said Mrs. Doolittle. "When I came here, I only wanted a place to call my own. Herbie's a love, really. Treats me like a queen, never asks about my past." She shifted in her seat, fiddling with the belt. "I wanted people to admire me, be special to them the way Bee and Nico are to everyone."

"How is holding Ivy against her will and making her work for you admirable?" I asked, then lit up one of Mrs. North's candy canes I found next to my seat.

"What do you mean, dearie? I admit I tricked her into letting me in the house and stealing the list, but I never saw her again. I don't go to the warehouse. That's Herbie's domain. Herbie would never hurt anyone. Ever."

"I saw her in the mailroom. She seemed afraid of that Edgemere man. He was hard on everyone." I turned to her. "Is that why you came tonight to the house? Did you want to read the letters I told you about?"

"It would break Herbie's heart if people were writing bad things about the company or him," Mrs. Doolittle said.

"I made that all up. Mrs. North knows you too well, it seems. She told me what to say and it worked."

"I never wanted to hurt anyone," Mrs. Doolittle said, her voice cracking. "Especially you, Natalie."

"That's not true. You wanted to hurt your sister and Nico, whether you admit it or not. You acted out of jealousy," I said. Turning my attention back to the road, I increased my speed. My relationship with Lady M and Felix played in my mind. Had I ever loved Felix or had some of my own actions been the result of jealousy?

Twenty minutes later, we were at The Everywhere Corporation. The Vespa was thrown to the ground and Holly stalked around the building, pulling on doors and beating on windows.

"No need for all of that," said Mrs. Doolittle. "I have the keys." She shook them in front of her. Holly and I followed her into the main reception area. Mrs. Doolittle flipped on a series of lights.

All the glass and steel reminded me of ice shining in the night. The room mimicked the photos of snow on Mrs. Doolittle's wall. Holly ran ahead of us.

"Where is she, do you know?" I asked, but Holly kept running up the stairs without answering. I followed.

"Dearie, I can't make it. You go on ahead. I'm taking the elevator."

On the second floor I found Holly standing next to Mrs. North and Nico. A young man, who I now recognized as one of the beautiful people from the glass office downstairs, stood next to Ivy. She sat at a table where it appeared she was carving some sort of vehicle from wood. Her leg was chained to the chair.

The man smiled at us. "Welcome to Santa's workshop where all the toys are made by elves," he said, then looked down at Ivy. "Well, at least one elf."

"Paolo, you're a horrible, horrible human," Holly yelled at Edgemere's son. "You were our friend and so helpful to Mr. Cl... North. Why have you done this?"

"Now, Holly, calm down. I promised you I'd find your sister, and as you can see, I kept my word. You can be with your sister. All you have to do is work for us."

Mr. Edgemere exited the office Mrs. North had searched. He held the elbow of a little, round man I assumed to be Herbie. "I'm sure we can come to some agreement here." Herbie was then shoved in a chair. "My son and I have been overseeing things here for quite a while. It was a pleasant surprise to learn that there was such a thing as elves. When Mrs. Doolittle here began pressuring her dearly beloved to take over the entire Christmas industry, we discovered there was really a North Pole and actual elves that made toys. True, we weren't prepared for the weather conditions and could never have survived there, but we could gather elves and have them work for us at the corporation. And when sweet Holly confided to my son that she and her sister were originally from a family of elves, I couldn't resist keeping an elf on the shelf, so to speak. Why go back to the North Pole when there are lovely little elves right here in Rehoboth?"

"Let her go," Holly cried. "It's all my fault. Let her go and I'll stay in her place."

"There will be a trade, you're right about that, but it will be you for Mr. Herbie Doolittle," Edgemere said as he looked around. "Where is Mrs. Doolittle? She must be here someplace."

I turned to Mrs. North, but she was no longer next to me. Nico also had vanished. Only Holly and I stood in front of Mr. Edgemere.

"And who are you?" Edgemere seemed to notice me for the first time. "You're too old to be an elf." He leaned closer and squinted. "Aren't you the woman who works at the candy store?"

He didn't recognize me from my previous visit, so I thought I might remind him. "No," I said. "I'm Kristina Kelly and I'm here to not only finish my report on the working conditions of The Everywhere Corporation, but I'm also a representative of the EWU. I must inform you that you are in violation of the worker's agreements. It's all going in my report."

He laughed. It was then I noticed the gun in his hand. "EWU? What on earth is that?"

I tried to keep my composure. "Elf Workers United," I said.

He pointed the gun at me. "Sit down. There will be no report." Edgemere gestured to a seat next to Ivy. "You can sit there, and Holly, you get over here next to your sister."

Herbie had said nothing this whole time. I could see the beads of sweat over his lip. He was visibly shaking. I walked over to the chair as directed. Holly followed me, but as she came closer to Ivy, she lifted her elbow and smacked Edgemere's son in the nose. I heard the crack. He doubled over as blood poured down his face.

From behind Edgemere, Mrs. Doolittle appeared. She grabbed hold of his wrist and bit him. Mr. Edgemere cried out in pain but managed to keep hold of the gun. I ran over and tried to snatch the weapon from him. We struggled; he was far stronger than me. I tried to hold on but could feel the gun slipping from my grip.

I heard a faint pop before feeling something sticky on my neck. I let go and dropped to my knees. Mr. Edgemere stood there in a daze. Glitter sparkled all around us. My shirt and hands were covered in purple ink and glitter.

"We don't allow weapons here," said Herbie, as sirens and blue flashing lights came to a halt outside the building.

Chapter 6

We sat in Mrs. North's living room. Holly served tea, but Mrs. North and Mrs. Doolittle had frozen Brandy Alexanders. Nico had talked Herbie into having a smoothie. Herbie made a face with every sip but managed to down the entire glass.

The police had arrested Mr. Edgemere and his son, Paolo, after an elderly couple called in a hostage situation. Ivy was checked over by the medics but didn't need any further care. She was keeping to herself in Mrs. North's office sorting the mail.

"I don't understand where you went or how Edgemere didn't see you," I said.

"You know why, Natalie," Nico said.

"No, really, I don't. One minute you were there, then you were gone. How did you get out without anyone noticing?"

"Years of practice," Nico laughed as he said this.

"Natalie, darling, it's always easy for us to move about without anyone really noticing. The only people that usually pay us any attention are the children. Mr. Edgemere would never see us for who we were, because he doesn't believe in us." Mrs. North topped her glass off with more of the frozen drink before offering the last of it to Mrs. Doolittle.

"He was too old to believe in Santa, is that what you're saying?" I asked.

"Age has nothing to do with it," Nico said. "He has never held the true spirit of Christmas. To him, the season is entirely about money."

Mrs. Doolittle turned to Herbie. "I'm sorry, dearie, for involving you in my grudge against my sister. Your motives were always pure. You only wanted to help make shopping easier for people. It certainly was a blessing to many over the last couple of years. I was greedy and saw nothing more than a way to get back at my sister. I truly didn't realize I was feeding into Mr. Edgemere's own plot to take over the season."

"I was weak," said Herbie. "I let success go to my head and let Edgemere convince me to let him handle things. Vi, you always did say I took the easy way out." Herbie stared into his now empty glass.

"I suppose it's back to the boarding house for me," I said looking at Mrs. Doolittle. "If my room is still vacant."

She and Mrs. North exchanged a glance. "We've discussed that," Mrs. North said. "I think Holly and Ivy should have the opportunity to see the world and spread their wings. They've been with us for years and need a chance to live like all other girls their age. Well, girls that look to be the same age."

"Yes, so Ivy and Holly will be moving to the boarding house and working the temp jobs until they decide what they truly want to do with their lives," said Mrs. Doolittle.

Mrs. North nodded. "And, if you agree Natalie, I'd like to offer you a permanent position as my personal assistant."

"There won't be anymore Christmas hostage situations that involve glitter guns, will there?" I asked.

"I can't make any promises," said Mrs. North, lighting a candy cane. "Crazy things happen around the holidays."

I only needed to think it over for a second. "I'd really like to work for you."

"I have an assignment for you," Nico said. "If you wouldn't mind. It seems I'll need a new Naughty and Nice List typed up. I have to make a few adjustments." He smiled at Mrs. Doolittle. "Hopefully, you'll behave yourself now."

"Cross my heart," she said, then did so.

"Come along, Natalie. There's much to do," said Mrs. North. "Once you've finished the list, we must look into this Santa bank robbery thing."

"I don't type, and I absolutely do not get involved with bank robbers," I said, following her down the hallway.

"I overheard the police discussing it. Seven men dressed as Santa have been holding up local banks. We can't tolerate that. I have a plan on how we can catch them. You're not going to like it at all."

I probably would hate it, but I'd go anyway. Mrs. North was right. Everything is permanent, but nothing stays the same.

The End

Also Featuring This Author

Shell House

Love on the Edge

Over the River and Through the Woods

Into the Woods

The Boardwalk

About the Author

KIMBERLY KURTH GRAY is a writer of fiction and memoir. She is the recipient of the William F. Deeck-Malice Domestic Grant, a Hruska Fellowship Finalist, and a Wellstone Emerging Writer winner. She lives in Baltimore with her family and her pampered pooch Romeo.

www.ingramcontent.com/pod-product-compliance
Lightning Source LLC
Chambersburg PA
CBHW030438120726
47903CB00003B/1014

9781646493043